Praise for *It's Always the Husband*

"Readers will be left in an adrenaline-inducing 'whodunit' game, until the completely unpredictable conclusion. This book is perfect for fans of Liane Moriarty's *Big Little Lies*."

—*Redbook* magazine (20 Must-Read Books for Spring)

"Demonstrating diabolical plotting chops and an ability to convincingly conjure settings, Campbell crafts a twisty page-turner." —*Publishers Weekly*

"*It's Always the Husband* has great character development, allowing readers to really get inside the minds of the characters until the very end, where a shocking twist leaves readers stunned."

—*RT Book Reviews* (Top Pick!)

"Riveting . . . keeps the tension high."

—Associated Press

"If you loved Liane Moriarty's *Big Little Lies,* put this thriller on the top of your list . . . you won't be sure 'whodunit' until the very (shocking) end."

—Today.com (Summer Beach Reads You Won't Want to Put Down)

"Excellent." —*New York Post* (Recommended Reads)

it's always the husband

MICHELE CAMPBELL

St. Martin's Paperbacks

IT'S ALWAYS THE HUSBAND

Copyright © 2017 by Michele Rebecca Martinez Campbell.

Excerpt from *A Stranger on the Beach* copyright © 2019 by Michele Rebecca Martinez Campbell.

All rights reserved.

For information address St. Martin's Press, 175 Fifth Avenue, New York, NY 10010.

Library of Congress Catalog Card Number: 2016050222

ISBN: 978-1-250-30941-9

Our books may be purchased in bulk for promotional, educational, or business use. Please contact your local bookseller or the Macmillan Corporate and Premium Sales Department at 1-800-221-7945, ext. 5442, or by e-mail at MacmillanSpecialMarkets@macmillan.com.

Printed in the United States of America

St. Martin's Griffin edition / May 2018
St. Martin's Paperbacks edition / April 2019

St. Martin's Paperbacks are published by St. Martin's Press, 175 Fifth Avenue, New York, NY 10010.

10 9 8 7 6 5 4 3 2 1

For my husband,
who has never tried to kill me . . .
as far as I know

I no doubt deserved my enemies
but I don't believe I deserved my friends.

—WALT WHITMAN

part
one

1

She stumbled through the dark woods, the trees dripping raindrops onto her hair and her party dress. Her shoes were covered in mud, and she trembled from the cold.

"Hey," she called out. "This is crazy. My shoes are soaked."

"Just a little farther."

She was out of breath, and her feet were killing her. It wouldn't be good for the baby if she tripped and fell. Then they rounded a bend. She got an open view ahead, and knew finally where they were. When she saw the ghostly shape looming in the distance, she stopped dead.

"*Why?*"

"You know why."

In a matter of minutes, they reached the foot of the

bridge. A frigid wind blew in her face, carrying the scent of decaying leaves and ice-cold water. There were barriers across the bridge now, blocking access, and a profusion of warning signs. *Danger. Private Property. No Trespassing.* The signs were there for liability reasons, but from what she understood, the local kids still loved to make the breathless leap into the river. The more people who died here, the bigger the dare. Kids had no fear; they were young, and didn't know better. She could have told them. Somebody dies, and it changes the lives of those left behind, forever.

"I don't know what kind of point you're trying to make, bringing me here," she said, her voice shaking with tears. But she didn't turn back.

They walked forward a few paces, stepped over an old, tumbled-down metal fence and kept walking until they got to where the center of the bridge used to be. There it was, the abyss that he'd fallen through, the night he disappeared forever. She looked down and saw the water roiling against the rocks. The town had done a crappy job of boarding it over. They'd "fixed" it many times in the intervening years, but they were too cheap for the one fix that would work, which would've been to tear the evil thing down once and for all. Below, the water swirled and foamed. She could hear the roar from up here, over the pounding of her heart.

"No," she said, backing away from the edge.

"Go ahead."

"Go . . . *ahead*?"

"Go ahead and jump. You know you want to."

2

Twenty-Two Years Earlier

Aubrey Miller lugged her heavy duffel bag through ivy-covered Briggs Gate and let it drop to the ground, stopped in her tracks by her first real-life glimpse of Carlisle College's world-famous Quad. It was a gorgeous late-summer day, and she twirled around three hundred and sixty degrees, drinking in the sights and smells of the place. Green grass, old brick, towering trees. The promised land. Aubrey had been dreaming of this moment ever since she'd picked up a Carlisle brochure in her high school guidance office back in Las Vegas three years before. Now, against all the odds, after three years of nonstop studying and scheming, here she was. Carlisle was more beautiful than she'd dreamed. Pictures didn't capture the place. The sense of peace that flowed from the mellow brick, the cheery shouts of the students as they greeted each other. Everywhere she looked, she saw students with their families—the Carlisle student identifiable by the expensive backpack, the well-heeled dad toting cardboard boxes, the pretty mom with a designer handbag, the gaggle of younger siblings. Aubrey was here alone. Her financial aid didn't cover her mother flying across the country to the East Coast just for the frivolity of unpacking her clothes for her and tearing up when they hugged good-bye. She told herself that was just as well. Her mother, who'd dropped out of high school when she had Aubrey's sister at seventeen, would never fit in. She couldn't imagine a place like Carlisle, let alone know how to behave here.

Aubrey settled the duffel bag back onto her shoulder and got her bearings from the campus map that she'd tucked in the back pocket of her jeans. Her dorm was called Whipple Hall, and it was located somewhere along this exquisite quadrangle. At one end of the Quad was Founders' Hall, with the famous statue of Elias Carlisle holding up the lantern of knowledge. Once she spotted the statue, Aubrey knew where she was, and within moments she was gazing in wonder at the graceful brick façade of Whipple, her new home. She couldn't believe she'd get to live here, after spending her childhood in a succession of crappy apartments with leaky sinks and dank hallways. It was a miracle.

The entry foyer was dim after the bright sunshine. Aubrey followed signs to Registration and ended up in the dorm common room, where she handed her driver's license to the cheerful lady behind the desk. As the woman paged through boxes of envelopes searching for Aubrey's registration materials, Aubrey took in her surroundings. Dark wood paneling, a fireplace with an elegant marble mantel, a sparkling brass chandelier. The common room furniture was cozy and well used; the bookshelves full of old yearbooks and board games. She'd never been in a place with this much history in her life, not where she came from. Tons of famous people had graduated from Carlisle over the centuries. Scientists, writers—presidents, even. She could visualize them lounging here in this very room, engaged in dazzling conversation. She imagined studying here herself, on a cold winter night in front of a roaring fire, talking about ideas, or just drinking cocoa with her roommates.

Roommates.

The thought of her roommates made Aubrey's stomach sink. At the beginning of the summer, the Housing Office sent her their names, addresses, and pictures, and invited her to get in touch. The purpose seemed to be to encourage cooperation about setting up the room—who'd bring the mini-fridge, who'd bring the speakers, that sort of thing. Aubrey had nothing more to contribute than the clothes on her back, but she wrote anyway, because she longed to know these girls immediately. From the pictures and the limited biographical information provided in the mailing, Aubrey had spent hours daydreaming about them already. The blonde with the perfect turned-up little nose, who lived on Park Avenue and went to a fancy private boarding school, was a debutante, Aubrey imagined, who owned a horse and played tennis. The brunette with the glasses and gold-cross necklace was quiet, studious, and religious. But maybe she was wrong, and anyway, she was dying to know more, so she wrote two long, chatty letters asking each roommate all about herself—about her family, her high school, her likes and dislikes, what she planned to study, anything Aubrey could think of, really. She'd mailed the letters two months ago now, and checked the mail every day for their replies. She'd never heard back, not a word.

Aubrey had been so focused for so long on getting into Carlisle, then on the financial aid, the plane ticket, and making money to help her mother get her bills straightened out before she left, that she hadn't thought much about how life would be once she got here. Whenever she did, the debacle of the roommate letters loomed, and made her feel sick to her stomach. It was surely her own fault that they never replied. Aubrey wasn't good at friendship. Back home, she'd been in the advanced placement classes, studying constantly whenever she wasn't working at whatever part-time job she could find. She didn't think of herself as ambitious, just as somebody who really needed to get out. Her mother worked back-to-back shifts as a waitress, her father was out of the picture, her older sister slept where she wanted to and didn't come home for days at a time. Aubrey became a reader early so she wouldn't feel alone in her apartment at night. Books kept her company and became her friends; they were more welcoming than people, and less threatening. In her school, there were kids who wouldn't come near her because her family was so-called white trash, and other kids who would give her the time of day but were into drugs, and sex and partying, and would only drag her down. Then there were the nerds like her, who would rather study than hang out.

The end result was no friends, and no social life. She didn't regret it. Look at the results. Here she was, eighteen years old, on the brink of realizing her dreams. But she didn't have a clue how to be a cool girl. No wonder the roommates hadn't written back.

All that was about to change. Her real life was starting. Whatever she'd done wrong before, she'd fix. If she'd been shy, she'd become the life of the party. If she'd been a nerd, she'd be the It Girl now. If she was skinny and gawky, she'd become thin like a model. No transformation was beyond her, not at this place. She'd make her roommates love her, no matter what it took.

The woman behind the desk handed her a packet.

"Key's inside, hon, suite 402," she said.

Aubrey thanked her and hauled her duffel bag out to the hall and up four flights of stairs. She stood outside the door to 402 for a minute, catching her breath and gathering her courage. As she rummaged in the envelope for her key, the door flew open, and a middle-aged woman rushed out, chattering in Spanish as she looked back over her shoulder.

"Ma, watch where you're going!" said a dark-haired girl, grabbing the woman's sleeve to stop her from plowing into Aubrey. "And speak English."

It was the roommate with the glasses, except she didn't have glasses anymore. Her pretty dark eyes and confident smile came as a surprise. She was intensely well groomed—perfect hair and makeup, cute capri pants and a starched white shirt—which immediately made Aubrey self-conscious about her crumpled traveling clothes and stringy hair.

"Jennifer?" Aubrey asked.

"It's Jenny, Jenny Vega. My mother was just leaving," she said.

The mother swept Aubrey into a bosomy embrace.

"*M'ija, cómo estás?* So happy to meet you. You come for supper Sunday, okay? I'm gonna make *pasteles*."

"She doesn't want to come for supper, Ma."

Aubrey actually did want to—the hug had brought tears to her eyes, which she blinked back as she untangled herself—but she suspected it would be better for her future relationship with the cool and uber-well-groomed Jenny not to say so.

"Why you so mean?" Mrs. Vega said to her daughter.

"I'm not mean. It's time for you to go, that's all. See you Sunday. Love you." Jenny kissed her mother dismissively and gave her a little shove.

Mrs. Vega marched away, grumbling, and Jenny held the door open for Aubrey.

"I'm Aubrey, by the way."

"I figured. No parents? Lucky you," Jenny said, looking up and down at the hall.

"I came all the way from Nevada, so—"

"Oh, right. You said that in the letter."

"You got my letter? Why didn't you—?"

"I just got it a week ago. I was away all summer at this outdoor leadership camp thing in the Adirondacks."

"Wow. Cool."

"It was pretty lame actually. Looks good on the résumé though. C'mon in, I'll give you the tour. You're the last to show up, so you get the dregs, I'm afraid, but still, it's nice. For a dorm room, anyway."

Aubrey picked up her duffel and stepped into an adorable living room. The suite was on the top floor, under the eaves, with hardwood floors and quaint dormered windows. She spun around, wide-eyed, taking it in.

"Cute, right? The sofa smells though," Jenny said, wrinkling her nose. Jenny herself smelled of some fresh, springlike perfume. "I can probably get us something better from my parents' store. I'm a townie, if you haven't figured that out by now."

"A—townie?"

"You know, town and gown? I grew up right here in good old Belle River, New Hampshire, which would be the armpit of the universe if not for Carlisle. Born in the shadow of the college, as they say. But my parents aren't connected to the college, far from it. They own the hardware store in town."

"That's awesome. I'm jealous."

"Jealous of growing up here? Hah, don't be. The college looks down on the townies, you know. Carlisle is a head trip. You'll see. The *people*—I'm telling you," Jenny said, rolling her eyes.

"What do you mean?"

"*Kate,* for example. She showed up first and grabbed the single, even though the housing letter says to wait and decide together who gets which room. So you and I are stuck sharing the double whether we like it or not. There's a lot of that around here. You know, people all full of themselves, stepping on each other."

"Maybe she thought we wouldn't mind sharing the double."

"Why wouldn't we mind? Of course we mind."

"Well, maybe she didn't think about it."

"Yeah, that's the point."

"I'm sure if we talked to Kate . . ."

"Oh, I tried. She just acted all vague and sweet, like she didn't understand what my problem was. Bullshit. She knew exactly what she was doing. She thinks the rules don't apply to her, and the fact is, they don't. She's Kate *Eastman,* you know, like Eastman Commons? Like *President* Eastman?"

"President—who?"

"Her grandfather or something, or maybe great-grandfather, was president of the college. Her father's a trustee. Their name is on *buildings,* you catch my drift?"

"She isn't here now, is she?" Aubrey glanced around in alarm, worried about being overheard, and getting off on the wrong foot with this exalted personage.

"Don't worry," Jenny said. "She ran off when I got in her face about the room assignment. But I'll shut up about that now. You must want to unpack."

"I don't mind, really. I'm just excited to finally meet you."

"Aw, sweet," Jenny said, and Aubrey heard a note of condescension in her voice. But she was probably being paranoid.

The double turned out to be a bright, spacious room with dormered windows and a skylight. Aubrey loved it but didn't say so, lest she appear uncool. Jenny was being so welcoming, and a misstep from Aubrey might turn her off. The double had two of everything— matching twin beds, two wooden desks with chairs, two bookshelves, two modular wardrobes. Jenny had taken the side of the room with the nook for the bed and slightly more space. (Aubrey almost said something about that; by her own logic, shouldn't Jenny have waited? But she held her tongue. Don't rock the boat.) Jenny's bed was made up with a lavender and white polka-dot comforter and piles of pillows in varying shades of lavender and purple. A bulletin board hung over the bed, crammed with colorful photos of Jenny with her friends and family. Over the desk, there was a second bulletin board, this one meticulously laid out with the orientation schedule and class list, all neatly highlighted in pink. The desk lamp had a shade that exactly matched the comforter cover, and under the bed and on top of the armoire, there were a bunch of cute plastic storage units—also lavender—that looked like they'd been hand-selected by an expensive decorator.

"Your stuff is so pretty," Aubrey said, taken aback.

It had never occurred to her how rich people would be here. Even the townie girl was rich. Every dollar of Aubrey's work-study money was earmarked for tuition. She'd better get a second job ASAP, if she wanted to keep up with these people.

Jenny's glance flickered over Aubrey's ratty jeans and old Chuck Taylors, and the army surplus duffel on the floor.

"Hey, you know, if there's anything you forgot to bring, you should let me know, because we have a lot of extra stuff at the store," Jenny said.

She wasn't trying to be unkind, but the pity in her voice was palpable. Despite herself, Aubrey entertained Jenny's offer for a second. The frayed sheets crumpled up in the bottom of her duffel were pretty awful. She'd love some new ones, and a few cute plastic storage units, too. But she wasn't a charity case.

"No thanks, I'm good," Aubrey said.

"Oh, hey, I meant as a loan. Seriously, you'd be doing my parents a favor. The room décor items sit around gathering dust and taking up space. Customers don't come in for them because it's mainly a hardware store."

"Thank you, that's nice of you, but I'm fine. I'm not into material things."

That was a lie, and a pretty obvious one, but Jenny had the sense to let it go. She helped Aubrey unpack her stuff, which didn't take long. Orientation festivities officially kicked off in a couple of hours with a band and a barbecue on the Quad. In the meantime they walked around campus checking people out, went to the bookstore (where Jenny bought a Carlisle sleepshirt with their class year on it that she charged to her account, the concept of the bookstore charge account coming as a revelation to Aubrey), and got iced coffees at a perfect, grungy café on College Street called Hemingway's that looked and smelled exactly how Aubrey imagined a café should. They headed back to the Quad just as the barbecue was starting. The scent of charcoal and burgers floated on the velvety late-summer air, along with an occasional whiff of pot. A band played a cover of "Peace, Love and Understanding." Kids danced, and laughed, and hugged, and lounged on the grass. A bunch of cute guys with no shirts tossed a Frisbee, egging on a goofy yellow Lab that kept jumping up and trying to snatch the thing in midair.

Every freshman dorm had staked out its own patch of ground, where it set up blankets and camp chairs. Jenny and Aubrey made a beeline for the Whipple banner.

"There's Kate," Jenny said, pointing.

A bunch of guys had gathered around a petite girl in sky-high platform heels standing under the Whipple sign. Aubrey only semi-recognized Kate from the picture. The image she'd carried in her mind all summer was of a snooty country-club brat, but Kate in the flesh was more hippie princess, with long flaxen hair and a ruby in her belly button. She had a wide smile and a throaty rich-girl voice that caught Aubrey's ear as they approached. When she saw Jenny and Aubrey, she immediately turned her back on her admirers and walked straight toward them.

"The roomies return!" Kate screamed joyously, holding out her arms. "I've been looking *everywhere* for you two! Gimme some sugar, my sisters!"

Kate stumbled over her platforms, practically falling into Aubrey's embrace. She was tiny, with delicate bones, and she smelled of herbal shampoo, and reefer. Aubrey put her back on her feet.

"C'mere, you," Kate said, and hugged Jenny, too.

"My God, you're wasted," Jenny said, and giggled.

"Too true," Kate said with a laugh, righting herself. Her face was flushed and her eyes were bright. "It's college! I am out from under the watchful eye of my keepers, and ready to party with my bestest girlfriends. They say your freshman roommates become your best friends for life. So—shall we?"

Kate crooked her arms. Jenny took one, though only after a noticeable hesitation; but Aubrey laughed out loud with sheer happiness as she grabbed the other. In that moment, Carlisle opened up to her like a flower. Kate gave off waves of light and energy. Colors seemed brighter and the air felt softer in her company. Most of all, arm in arm with Kate, Aubrey felt like she belonged, like she was free to live the life she'd imagined. No wonder she'd been such a loner in high school. She'd known somehow that this amazing girl was out there, waiting for her, and she hadn't settled for less. Kate was the friend she'd been waiting for her whole life.

3

"Jenny, you are *literally* a buzz kill," Kate said, over the whir of an electric fan. She paused with the match an inch away from the tip of the joint.

It was Saturday night, and classes started Monday morning. The three of them were draped across the new furniture that overflowed the cramped living room of suite 402. Jenny's father and brother had taken away the smelly couch and moved in a matching love seat and armchair upholstered in hot-pink suede. Kate immediately pronounced the new stuff "bourgeois," yet proceeded to lounge on it all afternoon in her cami-pajamas, with a cappuccino in a cardboard cup from Hemingway's perched on her bare stomach, talking on their shared room phone with some boy she knew from boarding school who was at USC now. (God, the phone bills the girl was racking up, that they'd probably have to chase her to pay, but it was impossible to stay mad at her.) The three of them were supposed to be getting ready to go out, but instead Aubrey felt marooned. They all did—weighed down by the heat, bathed in orangey-pink sunset that filtered through the skylight.

"Have it your way, then," Kate said.

She sighed and blew out the match. Aubrey admired Kate's delicate hands. Her chipped fingernails sparkled with sky-blue polish, and a spray of stars was tattooed on the inside of one wrist.

"I got all the way through high school without getting in trouble, and I don't plan to start now," Jenny said.

But there was no animosity in her voice. They were all lethargic, content to loll and idly chat. They'd been forecasting a thunderstorm, but it hadn't come yet, and the air coming in through the open windows was heavy and wet.

"Just for argument's sake, how exactly do you imagine we're going to get caught?" Kate asked.

"That fan does nothing to cover the smell. It blows it out into the hallway. I'm not judging you. Smoke if you want to, but if you do it here and the RA smells it, I'll get in trouble, too."

"That Asian girl? She would never rat us out."

"What does the fact that she's Asian have to do with it?"

"Nothing. She's some lowly biochem grad student. I could have her grant money pulled for looking at me the wrong way. Don't you understand what kind of protection you get by rooming with me?" Kate said.

"Well, I don't want that kind of protection. I don't agree with it."

"My, my, such an idealist," Kate drawled.

"Hey, it's after eight o'clock," Aubrey said. "Shouldn't we head out?"

They'd been through four deadly days of required orientation activities—team-building hikes, sexual harassment lectures, IT sessions where they learned to use Carly, the library's research database. Every night there had been pizza feeds, and bands, and open houses sponsored by some dorm or club. But tonight the true debauchery began. The first fraternity parties. Frat Row would be lit up like Times Square, and packed with hunky upperclassmen cruising for the tender flesh of freshman girls.

"If Miss Priss here is even coming," Kate said, but there was a note of affection in her voice.

"I'm thinking about it," Jenny said.

Aubrey sat up and reached for her sneakers.

"No you don't," Kate said. "Only geeks show up this early. And you're not going sober either. Not if you want to walk in with *me*. Where I come from, we pregame. Hold on a minute."

Kate got up and flounced off to her room.

"Have you registered for classes yet?" Jenny asked idly, considering her manicure.

"I thought we had until the end of next week," Aubrey said, sinking back down onto the sofa.

"Not if you want to take anything popular," Jenny said. "Popular classes fill up early. Tell me which courses you're thinking of, and I'll tell you if you should worry."

"I don't know. Maybe Renaissance Painting. Or Literature of the Outsider—I heard the prof for that is really amazing. Oh, and French New Wave Cinema, or Eastern Religions. There are so many."

Jenny frowned. "What do you do with courses like those?"

Kate came back, carrying a bottle of tequila and three paper cups.

"Courses like what?" she asked.

"Aubrey's thinking about taking Renaissance Painting and a bunch of other floofy stuff," Jenny said, smiling.

"*Floofy*?" Kate said, and laughed. "You're too much."

"You're saying those courses aren't practical," Aubrey said. "I get it, but why come to Carlisle if not to study things that inspire me?"

"Um, to get a job after?" Jenny said.

"What a bore," Kate said.

"Spoken like a girl with a trust fund," Jenny said.

"I swear, you are prejudiced against me, Jenny Vega, but I forgive you. Hey, I have an idea. I'll take Renaissance Painting, too, Aubrey. Then you can come to New York over break and we'll go to the Met and look at the paintings in the flesh," Kate said.

"Do paintings have flesh?" Aubrey said.

"Nudes do."

They laughed, pleased with their own cleverness. Kate sloshed a generous amount of tequila into each cup, releasing a bracing sting of alcohol into the steamy living room. Jenny made a face, which was a reaction to the smell of the alcohol, but Kate took it as a comment on her invitation.